pirism

10 □ Arm(s)
11 □ Leg(s)
12 □ Breast(s)
13 □ Nipple(s)
14 □ Anus
15 □ Genitalia
16 □ Internal Organs
88 □ Other (specify):

_____

5 □ Sawed Off
88 □ Other (specify)

_____

t

APPENDIX A:

an elaboration on the novel **THE END OF ALICE**

by A.M. HOMES

ARTSPACE BOOKS

SAN FRANCISCO

Book and Cover Design by Kristin Johnson

Evidence Photography by Kevin Noble

ISBN: 0-9631095-6-1

Printed in Hong Kong

Artspace Books are available to bookstores through our primary distributor:
D.A.P./Distributed Art Publishers, 636 Broadway, 12th floor, New York, NY 10012.
Telephone: 212/473/5119 or 800/338/BOOK. For personal orders, please write to:
Artspace Books, 123 South Park, San Francisco, CA 94107. Telephone: 415/546/9100
Fax: 415/546/0236.

Artspace Books are published by San Francisco Artspace, a nonprofit video production
facility, communication center, and publishing house.

The author would like to thank: Anne Marie MacDonald,
Maureen Keefe, Kristin Johnson, Sarah Chalfant
and Robert Johnson for their support and good advice.

APPENDIX A:

1. **His Confession**

2. **Physical Evidence**

Exhibit A: **Scrapbook**

Exhibit B: **Trinkets**

Exhibit C: **The Appropriate Forms**

3. **Sex Crime and Prison Punishment**
by Robert Johnson

SELF-PORTRAIT #1

8

1. His Confession

The summer I was nine my mother died. But before that happened something else happened, many things happened, and though I bore witness—and more—it was never clear to me what or why. I have forever played upon the sequence of that strange summer when time did literally change hands and the clock took to wildly spinning around. It would have been like a strange sweaty dream, a nightmare, except that when I woke, when the leaves turned and fall finally came around, I was alone. My life had been cleaved, irrevocably divided into a before and after.

That my family, my mother's family, never again mentioned her by name, never offered any explanation, was a detail I took as proof of my guilt, my own sick sense that I played a part in things. That nothing was offered kept me from asking, kept me convinced that they knew, they all knew—it was my fault. At nine, it did not occur to me that it might have been their guilt, the undeniable idea that something in their own actions had caused this horrible end. At nine, I was not so smart; I was only crazy with sorrow, furious that I'd been put up to such a thing.

Without even trying, without even knowing what was happening, without so much as an effort, in fact with only a plea, "No!"—a kind of pathetic begging, "No"—asking not to be brought into this, with nothing but my presence, my person, my love for my mother, I was drawn in, implicated. And despite my will—the will to remain who I was, as I was—there was confusion, uncertainty, the weakness of my person and then an unknowing of my will. And it did happen, it all happened. My desire confused itself and while I had once been sure that I had not acted, I became equally sure that I had—one often gets what one wants. Three weeks later, I became her murderer, or so I have always secretly said to myself.

If you want to know what led to what, how it came to be, I can only tell you my part. My story is mine only at times such as these when one must first take responsibility and then one's punishment.

So as not to go entirely around about it, backwards and forwards, confusing you as I so often confused myself, I will tell you what I remember. I will tell you what I've told no one else.

Wonder: Why do I draw you so close and pretend to trust? And it is pretend, a game, my game, played because I am so bored and desperate and beyond myself, because I have little to lose, because I have no one and nothing, because I am in this alone. Perhaps I am deluded, crazy to think that if I can make you understand, can recreate the events of a certain June and July, have you feel them as I felt them, then you will turn sorry for me, will do something for me, help me, relieve me. Perhaps you will then be willing to do what no one has ever done: exonerate and excuse me from this debacle that has become my life.

It begins with breakfast. Morning in June. I wake up, dress and go down to find my grandmother in my mother's kitchen, my grandmother hovering over my mother's stove.

"Over easy or sunny side up?"

"Up," I say, forever an optimist.

My mother's absence is not mentioned, is simply skipped over as though I might not notice. Through the day, silence builds. Unacknowledged, it multiplies. By dinner I feel I might explode. Within the rage is the frantic rumination that this day is a repeat of the morning two years before when I woke to find that while I'd slept my father had died. My father had died, seven men had been called, and while I dreamed they lowered him like a piano, eased him down the stairwell with a rope tied round his chest, his body too long and slowly going stiff to carry around the corners. And when I was told, I went to his room, thinking it wouldn't be true, thinking it a cruel tease, around the corner and through the door I found the bed stripped, the mattress bare and everything else in its place, as it was, as it should be.

That day and this day and over and over again, I curse God for my sleep, for so much lost at night, for the necessary slumber that deprives me of the events in my own life.

"Where's Ma?" I finally spit at supper.

"Charlottesville," my grandmother says. "Charlottesville," as if the name of a small southern town will tell me what I need to know. "It's a good facility," she adds. "They had my sister there once."

Facility for what?

Dishes done, she climbs onto a dining room chair, takes a suitcase from high in the closet, goes to my room and makes a swift transference of the contents of my drawers.

The bag is carried downstairs and set by the door, where it waits until morning when a horn blows outside and my grandmother picks herself up, pins on her hat and instructs me to collect myself, and pulls the door closed tight behind me.

In the middle of June I disappear. I am taken from my own life and set down in the home of the near stranger, who by some bit of poor fortune birthed the babe that is my mother. And there in my grandmother's house, I am given the same treatment of disdain and distrust that she'd previously reserved for her only child.

"There would have been others but the doctors advised against it," I heard her say. "Runs in families. Why make trouble when you've already got trouble?"

"How long will she be in Charlottesville?," I ask one morning.

"Well, that depends now, doesn't it?"

She squeezes the blood of an orange into a glass and sets it before me, thick with the meat of the fruit, with seeds I am afraid to swallow for fear a citrus grove will grow inside of me, its branches reaching up through my stomach into the back of my throat, tickling me.

"No seeds," my mother always said. "Spit the seeds."

In anticipation of the orchard within, I drink hesitantly. I cough and try to discretely spit the seeds into my hand.

"Swallow it," my grandmother says. "No one wants to see you regurgitating at the table."

I swallow and cough again. Frightened, I cough harder.

"And don't choke yourself."

"**M**y sister Sue was that way too," she says to her friends, like-minded women who spend afternoons in her living room, taking teas, rare-rooted brews they make themselves. There is a chorus to their discussion, an oft-repeated chant among the witches, "Crying shame. It's a crying shame."

"Sister Sue was that way too," my grandmother repeats.

"Crying shame. It's a crying shame."

Sister Sue, that way too. Round and round in my head, the echo, the incantation. What way? What way? Crazy like a loon. A loon?

I think of my mother, porcelain and milky glass, wandering, like walking and sleeping at the same time. Out the back door and into the woods behind the house, a white dress evaporating in the trees. She walks into the woods and returns hours later decorated with twigs, leaves, wild flowers, each hand carrying something she's found, oblivious to the cuts, scratches on her arms and legs. She comes out of it, rises to the surface and asks, "What happened today? I've already forgotten." I fill her in. I tell her what happened—but only to me; it seems pointless to tell the rest, pointless and unnecessary.

"Too much electricity in my head," she says rubbing her temples, "Too much."

My mother is the former Tomato Queen. Queen for a day in Morgan County, in the tiny town of Bath of Berkeley Springs, buried in the Mountain State, West Virginia.

"You and I," she says, a few days after she's back—we're still staying at my grandmother's house. "We'll take a little trip. We'll go back, to where I was raised, the old home."

My grandmother, bent over the oranges, elbow bearing down, shakes her head.

"It's not up for discussion," my mother says. "I'll have my boy with me, he'll keep me clean."

While she is out of the room my grandmother takes me aside. "Out of your sight," she says, "Don't let her out of your sight."

Somewhere near the fourth of July, the Tomato Queen returns to her hometown. She drives slowly, pausing on the outskirts to brush her hair, freshen her lipstick, to suck in the long deep breath that will glue her together. She eases her mother's Chevrolet into town, holding herself as if she expects the streets to be lined with well-wishers waving, a band of trombones and tubas waiting to play a certain pomp and circumstance.

We stop before we get too far, slide into a small parking place and I wait while Mama goes into a store, returning with a small brown paper bag tucked into her purse. We circle the family home, the house that was ours for generations—until Aunt Sue hung herself off the front porch for all the neighbors to see and my grandmother thought it best to relocate.

Mama stares up at the porch and says, "Some things are funny, aren't they?" Then we drive back into town and she walks down the street saying hello to every person she passes, acting as if they owe her some great greeting, as if she is still the Tomato Queen and this is still her day.

"A bath," she says to the attendant at the old Roman baths, "A great big bath."

The woman leads us down the hall to a room with a heavy wooden door. "You have an hour," she says, turning on the tub. Mama ushers me into the narrow room. The water is running.

"How much does it hold?" I ask.

"A thousand gallons," Mama says.

As wide as the tub and only a little longer, the room has a small space for the steps that lead into the water. There is a narrow chair and a thin cot dressed in a clean white sheet and that's all.

"Sometimes, it's just too hard, it's just too much," she says, sitting on the narrow chair. She takes off her shoes, reaches up under her dress and starts to roll down her stockings.

I sit on the cot and watch.

She smiles.

I am watching Mama, more than watching, looking.

"I'm so glad to be home. Missed you," she says, unzipping her dress, sliding it off her shoulders. "Thought about you three times a day."

She escapes her underthings and I look away. I've been looking too hard, looking instead of watching, looking instead of not noticing.

Her body continuously unfolds, a voluminous and voluptuous twisting, turning monument to the possibilities of shape, to the forms flesh can take. A body. A real body.

"Are you getting shy?" she asks. "Getting too old for your ma?"

My face goes blank, all feeling falls out of it. She reaches over and begins to unbutton my summer shirt, the one my grandmother pressed so stiff that it is sharp, painful in places. I raise my hand and take over the unbuttoning. I undress with the awkwardness of a stranger, wondering if this is the way things are supposed to be, if this is simply how it is done, wondering if my discomfort is my own peculiarity. I have no way of knowing.

Mama turns off the tub.

The Tomato Queen pulls her blond hair back, piles it high on her head and pins it there where it won't get wet. Strays trail down her neck. Her neck is damp, perspiration mixed with perfume, a sweet fruit, a strong liquor, the place you want to bury yourself, to drink. I kiss her neck and, with my lips pressed to her skin, inhale. Her neck seeps sweat. Teardrops afraid to escape her eyes sneak out the back and slip down her spine only to find her ass crack and be sucked back in.

Slowly, she descends the steps into the water. Her body, round, truly a pear, a plum and then some. The most beautiful woman, front and back.

Still the Tomato Queen.

She sighs, sweeps her arms wide, and splashes. "Heaven," she says.

I slip out of my underwear, leave everything folded on the chair and sit for a minute on the cot; naked, totally naked, so naked.

"You know," my mother says. "This town is where I met your father. Right here in this park, at a party for the Strawberry Festival. He towered like a tree."

She smiles. She's back. We will leave, we'll go home to our house and summer will start again. In my memory it is always summer. None of this will ever have happened. The bath will wash us, will clean us, erase everything and we will begin again.

I plunge in and swim to my mother.

"Your father loved it here. This was the one tub he could fit into. From the time he was ten or twelve he was just too big. He loved baths. Liked to soak."

My father was a giant, a true giant, seven feet eleven inches. It ran in his family. After he died, my aunt took me into her attic and showed me piles of clothing from the nineteen hundreds, all of it larger than life. "Always save the clothes of a big man," she said. "Their hearts don't last long, so big they wear themselves out. But save the clothes because every now and then there's a new one, and it's not like you can just go down to the store and outfit 'em."

"Why did you marry him?" I ask my mother.

"I always liked men," she says, as though that's an answer.

She leaves the bath, pulls the bottle from her purse and pours herself a glass. "Bathtub gin," she says carrying the glass back into the water with her.

In the water, she turns pink, she turns red. She lies back clutching the bar that goes the whole way around and like a ballet dancer doing her exercises, she opens and closes her legs. She teases me, making waves.

"Did I ever show you what having you did to me?"

16

I shake my head. She shows me her breasts. "I'm bagged out," she says, cupping them, holding them up, pointing them, aiming them at me like missiles. "Bombs away," she says. "You stretched me all out."

"I'm sorry," I say, horrified.

"Nothing to apologize for. It's my own damn fault."

She reaches for the bottle she's left by the side of the tub, refills her glass and drinks quickly.

"I'm frightened," she suddenly says. Her face has lost its color. She goes white, deathly white. "Give me a hug."

I go to her. Swim there. She pulls me against her. My cheek, my mouth, is at her breast. She flattens me against it and sees my embarrassment rise under the water.

Mama smiles and hugs me hard.

"Go ahead," she says, holding my head in her hands, turning it so that my lips are at her nipple. "If it belongs to anyone, it belongs to you." She moves my head back and forth over it. The softest skin, not skin but a strange fabric, a rare silk. My lips are sealed.

She rubs her finger over my mouth, "Open," she says. "Open up. It's only me, it's your Mama. Taste, just taste."

Like butter, only it doesn't melt. A tender saucer that pulls tight under my tongue, ridges and goose bumps.

She reaches for my hand. I try to pull away. "No."

"Yes," she says pulling harder on the arm, leading it toward the place between her legs.

"No," I say, more desperately.

My hand goes through a dark curtain, parting velvet drapes. My fingers slip between the lips of a second, secret mouth. My mother makes a sound, a guttural ahhh. I try to pull my hand out but she pushes it back in. Pushes it in and then pulls it out; pushes and pulls, in and out, in, out.

"It's your home," she says, one hand at the back of my neck, holding my head against her still, the other on my hand, keeping me there, her

17

leg wrapped around my leg.

"It's your home," she says again. "You lived there before you lived any-where else. You're not afraid of going home, are you?" she asks.

It grows slick, greasy with something wetter than water. My hand is inside my mother, in a place I never knew was there. Deeper. She takes three fingers and threads them into her. Perfume and juices, the cavern grows. She moves the hand in and out. My fingers are swallowed.

She grabs my arm at the wrist. "Fist," she says. "Make a fist, curl your paw." It doesn't go at first. Too large. "Push," she says. And I do. "Harder," she says. My knuckles round the edge of the bone and pop in. My fist is inside her. I turn it around, a screwdriver, a drill. I feel the walls, the meat she's made of, dark and thick. My fist is in and almost out and then in again. Her fingers dig into my bicep, she's controlling me. "Go," she says, deeply, desperately. "Go. More." She is pushing and pulling. I'm rocking, fighting. Buried in my mother I'm boxing. Boxing Mama, punching her out, afraid my hand will come off, afraid the contractions of her womb will amputate me at the wrist. My shoulder is stretching, nearly popping out and I can't stop, that much is clear. Whatever I do, I can't stop. She is filled with fury and frustration and there is no way of saying no.

She keeps my mouth at her breast. "Suck," she says, "bite it. It's yours." Harder and harder. Never enough.

And then with no warning, the teeth of this strange mouth bite my hand. Her head goes back and she bellows like I've killed her and I cry out too because she's hurting me and I don't know what's happening. I'm scared and I want my hand back and I want my mother back and I want to be out of this place.

It's over. As suddenly as it started. Mama holds up a hand, "Stop," she says. "Stop," she whispers in my ear. "It's enough." She puts her hand on my shoulder and tries to push me away but my fist is still inside her and suddenly I'm an intruder, a thief. I am doing something wrong. It takes me a minute, more than a minute. I've gone deaf, I don't catch on right away, I keep pulling and pushing and boxing, punching her insides, going the rounds, giving it my best. I'm doing my job, doing all I can.

"Stop," she says again loudly, the echo off the tile makes it sound like a shot.

I stop.

She reaches between her legs, plucks my hand out and lets it drop like some discarded thing. I've failed. I turn full front toward her and began to rub her, to poke at her with my skinny stub. She laughs and pushes me away, "Now you're just all excited. All riled up." She laughs as though it's funny. She gives me a kiss on the lips and climbs out of the tub, wrapping a towel around herself. She lies back on the cot, hand over her eyes and sighs, breathes heavily, deeply.

I'm staring, wondering what I've done wrong.

"Don't ogle," she says without even looking at me. "Swim some, get your flippers wet. "

I am still so small a boy that for me this tub is a pool. I take off, circling, turning laps and somersaults, I make myself relax, lose the cat o-nine tail that stood between us.

A knock at the door. "Hour's up."

Shriveled, I climb out of the water. My mother gets up, wraps me in a towel and I sit on the edge of the cot, resting while she dresses. I suck water from the towel and try not to look while she loads herself back into her costume.

"Don't worry," she says. "It's not to worry about. It's not you. It's not new."

She pulls herself together and leaves me to dress alone.

"Are you ready for lunch?" she asks as we step out of the bathhouse into the steamy July afternoon. "Let's have ice cream, ice cream all around. Six courses: milk shakes, ice cream sandwiches, spumoni salad, strawberry shortcake, pie á la mode and hot fudge sundaes."

The motel is cheaper than the inn. "Widow's got to watch her wallet." Mama pours herself a fresh glass as soon as we're safely in the room.

"My medication," she calls it. "I am a woman who needs her medication. Three times a day in Charlottesville, can you believe that, three times every day." She holds the glass out to me, "Here, take a taste, it won't kill you."

I shake my head.

"Between the sugar in the ice cream and this," Mama, says, tapping the side of her glass, "I'll be lucky not to go into a coma." She lies down on the bed. "A little nap. Just a little nap and we'll be all refreshed. Then we'll have dinner, Tom Turkey." She puts her head on the pillow and is asleep. In the bathroom I wash my hand and arm up to the elbow. Soap and water. Soap and water. I wash until I am burning red, until the skin is raw, until it can get no cleaner without being taken off, boiled and hung up to dry like Grandma's laundry.

My mother lies face down on the white chenille bedspread, her fingers reading the braille rose, the dit-dit-da dashing of Morse code, like a somnambulist. My eyes grow heavy and I lie next to her. Her arm hooked around me. Mama and her boy in a close knot. In the safety of her sleep, I sleep. When I wake she is in the bathroom with the door closed behind her. I can hear the whining of the hot and cold taps as much water is poured. Finally she emerges, renewed, her face portrait-pink, her dinner dress white silk, always white. She says it allows her to glow, allows her color to come out, her light to shine. I sit up. She comes at me with a wet comb. I stand and she tucks my shirt in, efficiently and expertly dipping her hands into my pants, tugging my tails all the way down.

"Did you sleep?" she asks. "Dream a pleasant dream?" She speaks as if singing, as if writing herself little lyrics, little lines.

I shake my head.

She seems fine, like herself, like she's always been, exactly as I remembered her. Me, it must be me, my stomach turns. It was I who slipped through God's graces and did such a terrible thing. My hand beats, pulses, throbs with the reminder and yet she seems without symptoms. I want to lift her dress, to snake my fingers, my eyes, into what lies in that lost location, searching to see if, beneath its protective costume, its mask, it is truly unaffected, unamused, or whether it is indeed weeping, seeping from the events. She acts as if everything is as it always has been, as if she is still my mother and I, her son.

We drive to the grand country inn, sneak up the stairs and then descend for dinner, sweep down the steps playing the game of paying guests. Everywhere there are men and women of opportunity and affluence, heroes and heroines who come here as George Washington did, to soak themselves, to let the waters work their wonders. Behind them trail the grandchildren; little girls with flowered dresses and boys in jackets and ties. Angry and ashamed, I tuck my shirt in tighter, sweep my hair over to the side.

As we go toward the dining room I feel the appetite of a carnivore rise, I smell juices dripping, can nearly suck the greasy grizzle, the bittersweet droppings of so many meats. It is as though I've been kept from my feed for lengths of days and nights although I quite clearly remember the glazed ham from the night before, the pineapple chunks, bright red cherries. But now the night before is the year before, the lifetime before, so much time has passed, so much has happened. I go into the dining room growling with the full hunger of a man.

Mama orders for me. When my plate arrives I can't hold my knife, can't grip it without crying, "my hand, my hand." Mama shushes me. Crippled, I will have to learn to write with a pencil between my teeth, a lick of lead steered by my tongue.

Mama clucks, then leans over and cuts everything into pieces.

"Can you manage now?" she asks, handing the fork back to me.

I nod. Flavor. Food comes alive in my mouth, on my tongue, more alive than I. The dull flesh of the turkey, stringy, as though one could shred a

bird, pull him apart string by string, the taut berry tang of cranberry com-
pote, stewed and soaked in lemon and sugar, a hearty woody walnut
stuffing with simmered mushrooms, carrots, celery and mixed nuts, the
high-rise biscuit filled with steam. I dip myself into the food, as though
I've never eaten before, never truly tasted.

And since that night, I have not taken the most pilgrim holiday, the
Thanksgiving meal, without conjuring the acts of that day, that out-of-
season afternoon, that simmering July, without wondering exactly what it
is one gives thanks for. Thanks that my life, my mortal soul was spared,
that in her merciless need, she didn't duck me under, dip me down below
the water line, and hold my head there while I sucked her, sucked water,
drowning me in her desire.

I fall far in love with my food, bewildered by my appetite, curious that I am
able to eat at all, to enjoy. But I do enjoy, pure pleasure in each fork raised
to my mouth. I am eating and loving it. I look around at the other people.
Right there at the table, I am growing, turning more complex. I push some
things down and let others come to the surface. There is no point to certain
things. I am different from these people and will always be different. I love
Mama and I hate them. I hate Mama and I love them. I love all of them and
Mama and I hate myself. I hate myself. I am a bad boy.

A man appears at the table. A big man, a large man with a belly and a
moustache, Santa Claus's brother.

"Can you bear for me to introduce myself?" he asks in long, drawn-
out tones.

Mama looks up, blotting her lips with a napkin.

"I'm Verell Reed from Lynchburg, Virginia. I'm an insurance salesman.
This hotel is something I insure."

Mama introduces herself, shaking the man's hand, "And this," she says
introducing me, "is my boy."

"And you're a fine boy. Why don't I buy you a hot fudge sundae. It's
not turkey dinner without dessert."

Mama and I look at each other. "No ice cream," we say simultaneously. He looks at us like we're crazy. I look away.

"Whatever you do, no ice cream," Mama says again.

I scream. You scream. We all scream.

"Join us for coffee," she says to the man. "Brandy," she calls to the waiter. My shoes are off. Under the table, my feet, my toes are rubbing the wooden floor. Everything is sensation. Mama dips her nose into the brandy glass. They talk. I don't listen to what they say. I am exhausted, broken off, floating. I am a boy, still a boy. Tired boy. Stunned boy. A boy who has just killed some part of himself.

The band begins to play. People start to dance.

"Shall we?" Verell ask my mother.

Her moment, her element. "Of course," she says.

Verell turns, puts his hand out to me," And you," he says "Do you dance as well?"

I don't answer.

"Like a prince," Mama says. "He dances like a prince." And they each take a hand and the three of us go onto the floor and I'm between them with my stocking feet on Verell's shoes and Mama's dress pressed against me. Like the middle of an Oreo, I am the cream. Verell presses closer to Mama and she's leaning into him, and soon there is no room for me. Verell and Mama take off, dancing, and I go back and put my head down on the table. I watch them through my water glass; small and far away like the wind-up couple on a music box. I close my eyes, I hear the music, the band is in my head. I sleep.

Someone is half-carrying me. We are in the parking lot.

"I could drive you back to your motel or we could go up to my room," Verell says. "I could get a cot for the kid."

"We'll be fine. It was a lovely evening, lovely to meet you, lovely to dance."

He kisses Mama on the cheek, tries to kiss her on the lips but she turns away, closes the car door, locks it. Verell blows drunken kisses as we back away.

"Alone at last," she says. "How horrible. How horrible that was. Are you sleeping? Are you in the land of dreamy dreams?"

"No."

I am awake. It is very dark, our motel is down the road ahead of us, the flaming orange "Vacancy" sign like a beacon drawing us home.

"Can you make it in all right?"

"Ummhumm." I trip over the curb, fall down. Mama laughs, thinks it is a joke, I tear my shirt and skin my palms, only I don't know it yet, don't know it until we get inside, into the light.

There is one bed, one big bed. I am beyond worry, care. I have no fear that what happened before will repeat itself. I strip down to my underwear and lie on the bed. The pillow is deep. I don't know who I am or where I am. The light in the bathroom is off. Mama, dressed in a nightgown, moves towards me, a ghost. She is in the bed and I am awake, suddenly awake, fully alert.

Her arm hooks around me "Sleep tight," she whispers.

No sleep, no rest. No slumber.

Mama and her boy in a close knot. Mama's arms at rest around me. In my arm there is a tingling, a clear memory of her on my fist, Mama fitted around me and me pushing harder and harder into her, against her. I reach beneath the blankets, and touch myself with my other hand. I lie awake until the sun comes up and then sleep in the seeming safety of early light until Mama kisses me, wakes me for breakfast and disappears into the bathroom.

The sheets are peeled back and in the middle of the pit where Mama had lain there is a bright blush of red, a thick streak of blood.

"Blood," I scream. "There's blood."

She is in the bathroom. I hear the whining of the hot and cold taps. My fault. All my fault.

"My curse," Mama says through the bathroom door. "It's my curse."

And then the door opens and she appears, fully dressed, made for the day. "Did you sleep? Dream a pleasant dream?" She asks again, still speaking as if singing. She is fine, like herself, like she has always been. Were it not for my sore hand, I would think it had not happened at all. I would think that it was something that had leapt out of me, a bit of my imagination. Me. It must be me. My stomach turns.

"Today," she says, "I'll go with the ladies and you go with the men. I need to be taken care of."

I don't respond, I have nothing to say.

"You look a little pale, do you need some lipstick?"

Her hand dips under her dress, her legs bow slightly, she pulls out fingers dipped in rust. She paints blood across my lips.

At breakfast I can't eat. The carnivore from the night before has vanished, withered and returned to its cage.

"We should go home. Grandma will wonder where we've been, what we're doing," I say, wanting a way out.

"This afternoon," Mama says. "After the baths."

It couldn't happen again. I wouldn't allow it. I would do something, I didn't know what.

Back to the park by the inn, the baths, the bubbling springs. This time at the other bathhouse, the one divided into male and female. I am relieved. I am taking a bath without Mama.

"Otis will be out for the boy," the woman behind the desk tells Mama.

"Be good," Mama says, going through the door marked "Women". "See you in an hour or so."

"Otis will show you the way," the woman behind the desk says, introducing me to a man dressed like a baker, all in white. "His ma's next door," the woman tells Otis. Otis blinks. He is skinny and bald, not a twig of hair on him. On his arm is a green tattoo—a woman in a grass skirt. Except for the tattoo, everything, including his shoes, is white.

I follow him through a door. Naked men. I've never seen naked men before. It is worse than I could have imagined. I want Mama, I don't care what she makes me do.

"Put your clothes in here," Otis says, showing me a locker. "I'll get your bath."

Naked, everyone except Otis is naked. I am a boy, a small boy, a baby boy, clean and white. Dark monsters. I look at them, at the mats of hair from where they come, the bellies that drop down over them. I hope it will never happen to me. The way I am. I want to be the way I am for the rest of my life.

Otis takes me to my tub. It is a regular bath, narrow and long. I lie in the water; it is warm. I can see other men in their baths, men in the middle of the room being pounded on by men like Otis, men in white, who plunge their hands into flesh and knead it like dough. The men lie there taking it, blank-faced. Their eyes are closed. It is best not to watch. I shut my eyes.

Otis comes for me. "Can't have you shrivel up, what would your ma say." I climb out of the tub and he wraps me in a sheet, makes me into a mummy and takes me down the hall to an empty room filled with cots. "Pick one," Otis says. "Take a rest. Don't worry, I won't forget you."

I lay on the cot. Because I didn't sleep the night before, because the bath was so warm, because I have been so afraid and now am alone, I relax, I fall into a deep sleep.

A man comes up behind me, touches me. At first, because I think it is the same as what I saw in the other room, I do not say anything. I keep my eyes closed as though I am still sleeping. He rubs his hands over me, taking the sheet down. He touches and pretends not to touch. He is over me and he is on me. I am being laid upon. Poof, like a sofa cushion. I can't breathe. I try to turn my head but can't. There is something bristly on my neck, feathers or pins, bristle. There is so much of him, he is so large, that he pours out over me, over the edge of the cot. I am trying to keep my head up, to keep my head from being pressed into the pillow. It is all I can do. If I could breathe, I would scream. His arms are on either side of me, they are thick and hairy—there is no tattoo. He is on me. I can feel the heat of his cock, his thick and ready worm. I hold myself, clenched closed and tight. He is kissing the back of my neck, humping my ass. I cannot breathe. I faint. I feel myself falling away.

I don't remember more. Otis has me by the shoulders, shaking me, waving something strong under my nose. "Don't tell your ma, kid, whatever you do, don't tell your ma. I must have left you in for too long. Did you have anything to eat today? Did you have breakfast? Here, eat this." A candy bar, chocolate and caramel and nuts. He holds a glass of water for me. "Drink," he says. "Drink some more, swallow. Haven't ever had a kid go out on me like that before. You really scared me. Scared me." Otis helps me dress and I sit in the office with him until he is sure I won't faint again, won't fall out from under, then he lets me go. I run. I run out of the building and into the park. It is a sunny day. A bright and sunny day. The sun is high. There is a pool in the middle of the park. There are children in the pool. I watch them. I run up and down the length of the fence that goes around the pool. I am running and barking like a dog.

Mama comes. She comes out of the bathhouse looking radiant. She buys us ice cream and we sit on a bench looking at the pool, the park, and back at the bath house.

A man comes out, a big man with a moustache, Verell Reed. Mama waves. He looks at us, flushes red, then turns and hurries away. I begin to cry. The ice cream falls off the cone.

"Don't worry," Mama says. "There's always more, there's always more where that came from."

I am crying, weeping, wailing. People are beginning to watch, to wonder. Mama tells me to stop. I can't stop. There is no going back. Mama takes me to the car and we drive back to Grandma's house. I cry the whole way home.

"Stop," Mama says, "Stop, you're driving me over. Stop, boy, stop. You're driving me."

Mama is dead.
The telephone rings, Grandma answers it, listens then hangs up, turns to me and says, "She went over, off the road at the panoramic view, by the steakhouse. She's dead."

A bomb has been dropped. We're all dead only I don't know it yet. There is nothing left. I am alone, all alone. She has left me here with this woman who will keep me only because it would be more embarrassing not to.

The howling begins. A wail. A siren that never goes off, only grows distant and then more near, a siren that warbles within me, deafening me. And when they ask, I tell them I am an orphan raised from birth by my grandmother, my mother's mother. Orphan.

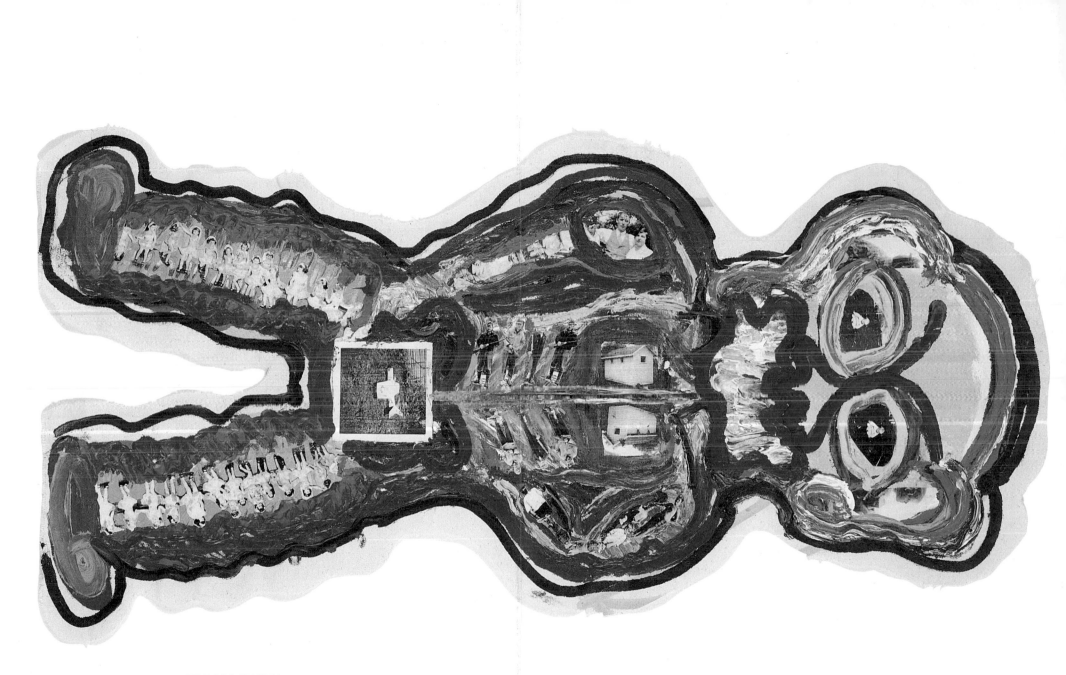

SELF-PORTRAIT #2

PORTRAIT OF ALICE #1

30

2. Physical Evidence

Exhibit C: The Appropriate Forms

Kittens behind the house

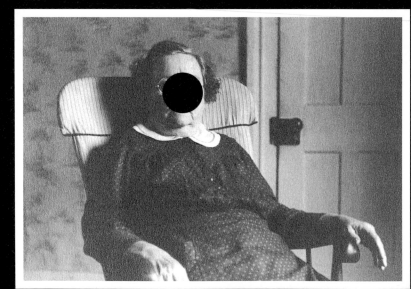

family outing, Virginia Beach, Virginia

mother

mother and father before i was born

athhouse, Beverly Springs W. Virginia

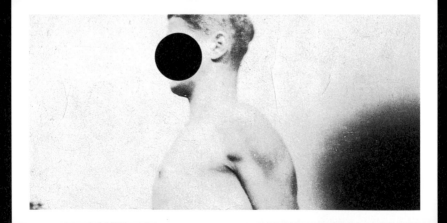

Father when he was young

1816 Spruce Street (Grandmother's House)

This is where some of the worst things happened

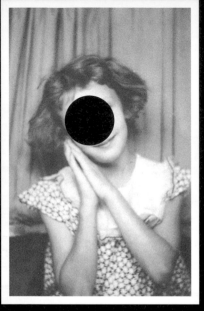

Alice (wishful)

On my way out
(I took this picture myself)
Richmond, Va.

My hiding place

sailor (with one in the hand)

Alice

My new coat, Philadelphia

37

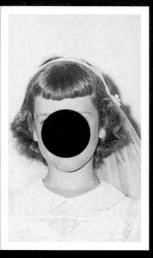

Alice (communion photo)

Alice's white shoes (Philadelphia

Linden Road, Scarsdale

Alice's tree in full bloom

Cabin, New Hampshire

At the cabin, August 1971

Prison near Albany (My current residence)

fishing boy (upstate, 1965)

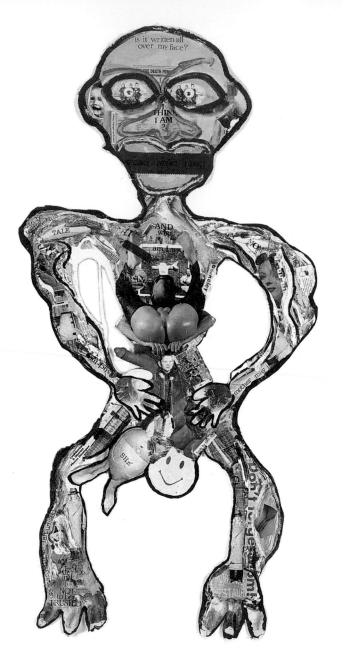

SELF-PORTRAIT #3

2. **Physical Evidence**

Exhibit B: **Trinkets**

ITEM #2 CHILD'S WATCH

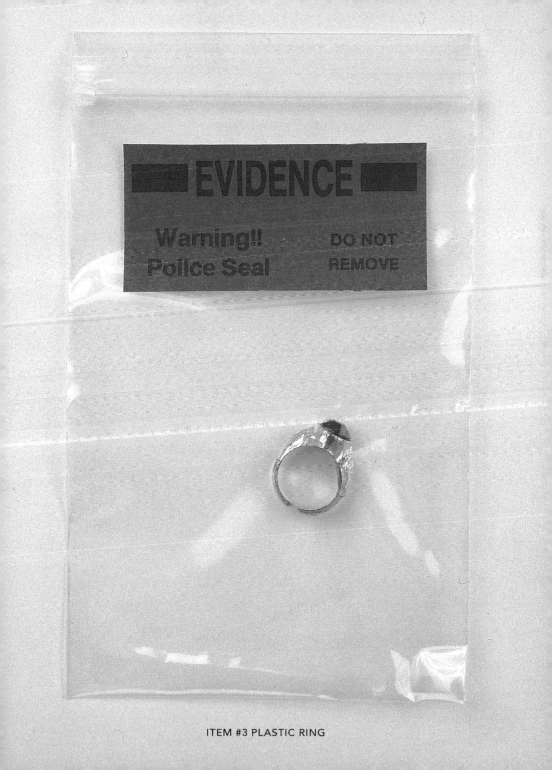

ITEM #3 PLASTIC RING

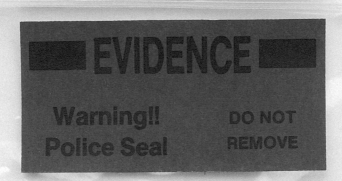

ITEM #5 THREE TEETH

ITEM #20 SMILE BUTTON

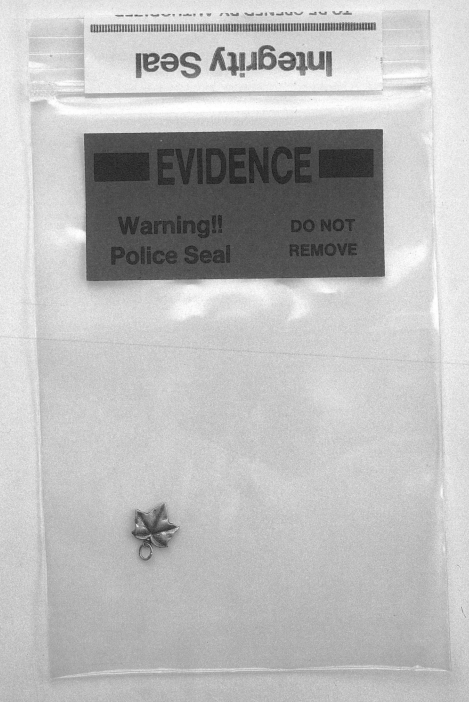

ITEM #28 CLAYTON'S IVY LEAF

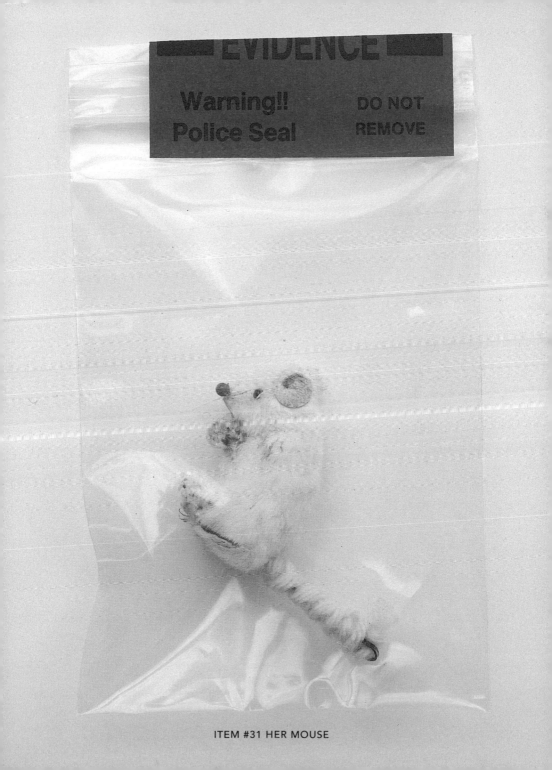

ITEM #31 HER MOUSE

SELF-PORTRAIT #4

2. Physical Evidence

Exhibit A: **Scrapbook**

LEASE AGREEMENT

The parties agree as follows:

DATE OF THIS LEASE:

PARTIES TO THIS LEASE:

Landlord: May 10 19 71

Address for notices:

Virginia Somerfield
Back Pond, Ossipee NH

Tenant: ▓▓▓▓▓▓▓▓▓▓▓▓▓▓

Address: ~~1744 Chestnut Street, Philadelphia PA.~~

TERM:

1. The Term of this Lease shall be ~~XXXXX~~ for 3 ~~month~~ beginning May 2 0 19 71
ending September 5 1971

PREMISES RENTED:

2.

USE OF PREMISES:

3. The Premises may be used as a living place for persons only.

RENT:

4. The rent is $750.00 on signing payable as follows:

Landlord need not give Tenant notice to pay rent. Tenant must pay the rent in full and not subtract any amount from it.

SECURITY:

5. Tenant has given Landlord $ 220.00 as security. If Tenant fully complies with all of the terms of this Lease Landlord will return the security after the Term ends. If Tenant does not fully comply with the terms of this Lease, Landlord may use the security to pay amounts owed by Tenant, including damages.

UTILITIES AND SERVICES:

6. Tenant must pay for the following utilities and services when billed:
~~gas, water, electric, fuel,~~ telephone, ~~gardening~~

These charges will be added to and payable as rent.

FURNISHINGS:

7. If the Premises are furnished, the furnishings shall be the items listed in "Schedule A" attached to this Lease. The furnishings shall be in good repair when Landlord gives possession.

REPAIRS. ALTERATIONS:

8. Tenant must keep, and at the end of the term return the Premises and all appliances, equipment, furniture, furnishings and other personal property clean and in good order and repair. Tenant is not responsible for ordinary wear or damage by the elements. If Tenant defaults, Landlord has the right to make repairs and charge Tenant the cost. The cost will be added to and payable as rent. Tenant must not alter, decorate, change or add to the Premises.

LANDLORD MAY ENTER, SIGNS:

9. Landlord may at reasonable times, enter the Premises to examine, to make repairs, and to show it to possible buyers, lenders or tenants. Landlord may place the usual "For Rent" or "For Sale" signs upon the Premises.

COMPLIANCE WITH AUTHORITIES:

10. Tenant must, at Tenant's cost, promptly comply with all laws, orders, rules and directions of all governmental authorities, property owners associations, insurance carriers or Board of Fire Underwriters or similar group.

COOKING:

11. Tenant may cook only in the areas specially set aside by Landlord for cooking.

CARE OF PREMISES, GROUNDS:

12. Tenant must not allow anyone to bring in dirt or sand, nor enter the Premises in wet clothing. Tenant must use special areas provided for showering and dressing after outside activities. Tenant shall keep the grounds neat and clean. Vehicles may be driven or parked only in driveways or in the garage.

FIRE, DAMAGE:

13. Tenant must give Landlord immediate notice in case of fire or other damage to the Premises. Landlord will have the right to repair the damage within a reasonable time or cancel this Lease. If Landlord repairs, Tenant shall pay rent only to the date of the fire or damage and shall start to pay rent again when the Premises become usable. Landlord may cancel the Lease by giving Tenant 3 days' written notice. The Term shall be over at the end of the third day and all rent shall be paid to the date of the damage.

NO LIABILITY:

14. Landlord shall not be liable for injury or damage to Tenant or to any person who uses or is on the Premises, or be liable for damage to their property, unless it results from Landlord's negligence. Tenant is responsible for all acts of Tenant's family, employees and persons Tenant invites onto the Premises.

LANDLORD'S CONSENT:

15. If Tenant requires Landlord's consent to any act and such consent is not given, Tenant's only right is to ask the Court to force Landlord to give consent. Tenant agrees not to make any claim against Landlord for money or subtract any sum from the rent because such consent was not given.

ASSIGNMENT, SUBLET:

16. Tenant may not sublet all or part of the premises, or assign this Lease or permit any other person to use the Premises.

TENANT'S DEFAULTS:

17.a Landlord may give 5 days written notice to Tenant to correct any of the following defaults:

    17.a.1 Failure to pay rent or added rent on time.

    17.a.2 Improper assignment of the Lease, subletting all or part of the Premises, or allowing another to use the Premises.

    17.a.3 Improper conduct by Tenant or other occupant of the Premises.

    17.a.4 Failure to fully perform any other term in the Lease.

17.b If Tenant fails to correct the defaults in section 17.a within the 5 days, Landlord may cancel the Lease by giving Tenant a written 3 day notice stating the date the Term will end. On that date the Term and Tenant's rights in this Lease automatically end and Tenant must leave the Premises and give Landlord the keys. Tenant continues to be responsible for rent, expenses, damages and losses.

LANDLORD'S REMEDIES:

17.c If the Lease is cancelled, or rent or added rent is not paid on time, or Tenant vacates the Premises, Landlord may in addition to other remedies take any of these steps:

    17.c.1 Enter the Premises and remove Tenant and any person or property;

    17.c.2 Use dispossess, eviction or other lawsuit method to take back the Premises.

17.d If the Lease is ended or Landlord takes back the Premises, Landlord may re-rent the Premises and anything in it for any Term. Landlord may re-rent for a lower rent and give allowances to the new tenant. Tenant shall be responsible for Landlord's cost of re-renting. Landlord's cost shall include the cost of repairs, decorations, broker's fees, attorney's fees, advertising and preparation for renting. Tenant shall continue to be responsible for rent, expenses, damages and losses. Any rent received from the re-renting shall be applied to the reduction of money Tenant owes. Tenant waives all rights to return to the Premises after possession is given to the Landlord by a Court.

18. If Tenant fails to correct a default after notice from Landlord, Landlord may correct it for Tenant at Tenant's expense. The sum Tenant must repay to Landlord will be added to and payable as rent.

WAIVER OF JURY, COUNTERCLAIM, SET OFF:
19. Landlord and Tenant waive trial by a jury in any matter which comes up between the parties under or because of this Lease (except for a personal injury or property damage claim), In a proceeding to get possession of the Premises, Tenant shall not have the right to make a counterclaim or set off.

ILLEGALITY:
20. If any part of this Lease is not legal, the rest of the Lease will be unaffected.

NO WAIVER:
21. Landlord's failure to enforce any terms of this Lease shall not prevent Landlord from enforcing such terms at a later time.

NOTICES:
22. Any bill, statement or notice must be in writing and delivered or mailed to the Tenant at the Premises and to the Landlord at the Address for Notices. It will be considered delivered on the day mailed or if not mailed, when left at the proper address Any notice must be sent by certified mail. Landlord must send Tenant written notice if Landlord changes the Address for Notices.

SUB-ORDINATION:
23. This Lease and Tenant's rights are subject and subordinate to: all leases for the Premises or the land on which it stands, mortgages on the leases or on the Premises or on the land, money paid or to be paid by the lender under mortgages, and changes of any kind in and extensions of such mortgages or leases whether now or in the future. Tenant must promptly execute any certificate(s) that Landlord requests to show that this Lease is subject and subordinate.

MARGIN HEADINGS:
24. The margin headings are for convenience only.

BROKER:
25. The Landlord hereby recognizes

as the Broker negotiating this Lease and agrees to pay the commission to said Broker. The Landlord shall pay a commission upon renewal of this Lease on the same or different terms, or upon the sale or exchange of the Premises between the parties. Commissions shall be paid as follows:

and shall be due and payable on execution and delivery of this Lease, renewal of lease, contract of sale or of exchange.

QUIET ENJOYMENT:
26. Landlord agrees that if Tenant pays the rent and is not in default under this Lease, Tenant may peaceably and quietly have, hold and enjoy the Premises for the Term of this Lease.

SUCCESSORS:
27. This Lease is binding on all parties who lawfully succeed to the rights or take the place of the Landlord or Tenant.

CHANGES:
28. This Lease can be changed only by an agreement in writing signed by the parties to the Lease.

LEASE FOR NEW HAMPSHIRE CABIN

SIGNATURES:
The parties have entered into this Lease on the date first above stated.

Landlord: _____
Virginia Somerfield

Tenant: _____

Witness: ....

GUARANTY OF PAYMENT

DATE OF GUARANTY:
19

GUARANTOR AND ADDRESS:

REASON FOR GUARANTY:
1. I know that the Landlord would not rent the Premises to the Tenant unless I guarantee Tenant's performance. I have also requested the Landlord to enter into the Lease with the Tenant. I have a substantial interest in making sure that the Landlord rents the premises to the Tenant.

GUARANTY:
2. The following is my Guaranty:
I guaranty the full performance of the Lease by the Tenant. This Guaranty is absolute and without any condition. It includes, but is not limited to, the payment of rent and other money charges.

In addition, I agree to these other terms:

CHANGES IN LEASE HAVE NO EFFECT:
3. This Guaranty will not be affected by any change in the Lease, whatsoever. This includes, but is not limited to, any extension of time or renewals. The Guaranty will bind me even if I am not a party to these changes.

WAIVER OF NOTICE:
4. I do not have to be informed about any default by Tenant. I waive notice of nonpayment or other default.

PERFORMANCE:
5. If the Tenant defaults, the Landlord may require me to perform without first demanding that the Tenant perform.

WAIVER OF JURY TRIAL:
6. I give up my right to trial by jury in any claim related to the Lease or this Guaranty.

CHANGES:
7. This Guaranty can be changed only by written agreement signed by all parties to the Lease and this Guaranty.

SIGNATURES:
GUARANTOR: ....

WITNESS: ....

She's sleeping, dozing in the passenger seat. I
write as i drive, diary propped on the dash. W
speed towards New York. Gram has had a str
and she, herself, a tantrum. it's a long story,
but i'm glad to have her back, even though
things are strained, how glad i am. i couldn't
stand the absence. Yet, i am overwhelmed wit
kind of sick sensation, a spinning hatred. She is
changing. i have denied it, but she is leaving
Going, going gone. She has lost the ring--the ri
gave her after our first date." i lost the ring
the lake," she says, referring back to the
episode, the heart stopping histrionic hi-jinks th
spurred our separation. "Does that mean we're
divorced? you must hate me," she says. No.
Well, i hate you." And so we are off, she
being a complete tyrant--purposely punishing
t is getting worse and yet i am glad for it,
ure i deserve it. Terrified, terrorized-- soon it
will end. Hoary Elfin.

itful sleep. 7:30 a.m. Central Park. Bethesda
ountain. doused in spray. I am free. Left the
ittle rat and her raunchy rat pack at the
laza. still a-slumber in their tombs. My min
uns on. skipping from thing to thing. un-twisted.
n-tied. giddy. grateful to be gone. The world
s filled with possibilities. I write from the
asis coffee shop - Columbus near 86th. The
aitress hovers--my tongue tingles from the
acon salt--she refills my coffee. My hand
overs the page. I am so relieved things ended
here they did--my ruby. my pearl is safe in h
other's hotel suite. I feel badly at having
ade my exit. so rude and raw--leaving withou
aying good-bye. but frankly. I was afraid to
ee her again. Today. I leave the city. leave no
nowing where I am going. only knowing that I a
one. Released. relieved. Yesterday and the day
before I had the feeling that something
orrible might happen. some storm might rise. an
ight escape myself in some unforgivable way
--lucky to have gotten out alive.

Statement of (Name) ▓▓▓▓▓▓▓▓	Complainant/Victim Name Alice Somerfield
Address ▓▓▓▓▓▓▓▓	Address 72 Maple Terrace Scarsdale, New York
Age ▓▓ DOB ▓▓ ▓▓	Classification Kidnapping/Murder
Res. Phone 2I#-757-6566 Bus. Phone n/a	Date of Occurrence August 8, I97I
Location of Interview Chatham Station	

I, ▓▓▓▓▓▓▓▓▓▓▓▓▓▓▓▓ , do freely and voluntarily provide the following statement:

Leaving New York at approximately 5:45 p.m on August 8, 1971 I drove North on the Henry Hudson, Saw Mill and Taconic Parkways, stopping at The Chatham Motel--I saw the vacancy sign from the Parkway. Checking in, I asked for the name of a local restaurant and was referred to Tree Top House, a steak joint with a view. I took a table, placed my order--meat loaf and mashed--and went to wash my hands. When I returned Alice Somerfield was at my table, eating my dinner. She said she had been hiding in my car all afternoon--sure I would leave New York without her--she called me names; "Liar, Speed Demon, Dirty Old Man," and attempted to induce me to having sex relations with her at the table using several key pieces of silverware; a fork, a knife, a spoon. She then ate my dinner, and a cup of tea and slice of apple pie a la mode and we went back to the motel, where Alice claimed to not feel well. She went into the bathroom, and given her mood, I worried that she might harm herself. "Alice," I called through the door. "Alice, is everything all right?" She returned, "I'm bleeding," she said, dipping her hands under her dress. When I attempted to explain that this was simply the start of her monthlies, a struggle ensued, during which Alice produced a knife, threatening me with it. "You've killed me," she said. I wrestled with her. "I don't want to hurt you," I said. "Then why did you do this?" She said. I had no answer "Why did you do this?" she said. "Why do you make me." And subsequently she was injured. Again and again. When she was calm, I went outside. I smoked. There was thunder and lightening, a storm. I stayed outside until the cleaning lady, Mrs. Juanita Watson, came with her cart at approximately 7:37 a.m.. I was greatly relieved to see Mrs. Watson, even though we'd never met before. I saw her and felt that she would go into the motel room and she would make everything all right again.

There's really nothing else to say, except that while I accept responsibility for the events--being that I am the elder--I must also add that Alice herself, with a penchant for certain forms of what can only be called S&M was an active participant--at times almost asking for it. I hope you don't think it odd that I say that now, that I add that as a twist.

I have read this statement prepared by Detective W. Reese , which consists of I (typewritten) (handwritten) pages, and have been given the opportunity to make corrections thereon. I attest that this statement is true and correct, to the best of my knowledge, and that I gave this statement freely and voluntarily without coercion or promise of reward.

Signed: ▓▓▓▓▓▓

Date: Aug 9, I97I Time: 3:40 p.m.

Witnessed by: ▓▓▓▓▓ Date: August 9, I97I Time: 3:54 p.m.

Investigated: ▓▓▓ William Reese Date: August 9, I97I 3:55 p.m

STEP 2 VICTIM'S MEDICAL HISTORY AND ASSAULT INFORMATION
(PLEASE PRINT)

1. Victim's Name: __Alice Somerfield__

2. Date of Birth: __5/20/59__   3. ☐ Male ☒ Female 4. Race: __caucasian__

5. Marital Status: ☒ Single ☐ Married ☐ Separated ☐ Divorced ☐ Widowed

6. Date and time of the alleged assault: __8__ / __8__ / 19 __71__   __10-11 P.M__ AM/PM

7. Date and time of the hospital examination: __8__ / __9__ / 19 __71__   __12:00noon__ AM/PM

8. Examining physician: __Dr. Wilfred Adler__   9. Nurse: __Cynthia Thomas__

10. Between the assault and now, has the victim:
    - ☐ Bathed/Showered
    - ☐ Douched
    - ☐ Brushed Teeth
    - ☐ Used Mouthwash
    - ☐ Changed Clothes
    - ☐ Urinated
    - ☐ Defecated
    - ☐ Vomited
    - ☐ Drunk

	Attempted	Successful	Ejaculation	Yes	No	Unsure
11. Was there penetration of the: **Vagina**	☐	☒	☒	☒	☐	☐
Anus	☐	☒	☒	☒	☐	☐
Mouth	☐	☒	☒	☒	☐	☐

12. Oral/Genital Sexual Contact: ☒ Fellatio ☒ Cunnilingus

13. Did assailant use: ☐ Lubricant ☐ Condom ☒ Insert foreign object(s) __Hunting Knife aprox 6in.__

	YES	NO
14. Was the victim menstruating at the time of the assault?	☒	☐
15. Any consensual coitus in the last 72 hours?	☐	☐ unknown

If Yes, Date: _____ and Time: _____

If Yes, was a condom used? ☐ YES ☒ NO

16. Is the victim pregnant? ☐ YES ☒ NO

If Yes, duration of pregnancy: _____

17. Any injuries to the victim resulting in bleeding? ☒ YES ☐ NO

If Yes, describe __multiple stab wounds, anal lacerations.__

18. Number of assailants: __one__

19. Race of assailant(s) if known: __caucasian__

20. Assailant(s) relationship to victim:
☐ Stranger ☒ Acquaintance ☐ Relative (specify): _____

21. Any injuries to the assailant(s) resulting in bleeding? ☐ Yes ☐ No ☒ Unsure

If Yes, describe: _____

22. Was any medication taken by the victim prior to or after the assault? ☐ Yes ☒ No

If Yes, describe: _____

23. Was any coercion used? ☒ Yes ☐ No

If Yes, ☒ Knife ☐ Gun ☐ Choke ☐ Fists ☐ Verbal Threats

☐ Other: _____

24. Emotional demeanor of the victim; i.e., crying, angry, agitated, lethargic, frightened, shocked, depressed, etc. __Dead.__

25. Description of the victim's outward appearance; i.e., clothes torn, shoe(s) missing, etc.: __nude except shoes &socks;handwriting on bottom of left shoe__

"Out of the ash I rise with my red hair and I eat men like air."

26. Victim's description of the alleged assault: __Victim unable to describe.__

Signature of Examining Physician   8/10/71 Date

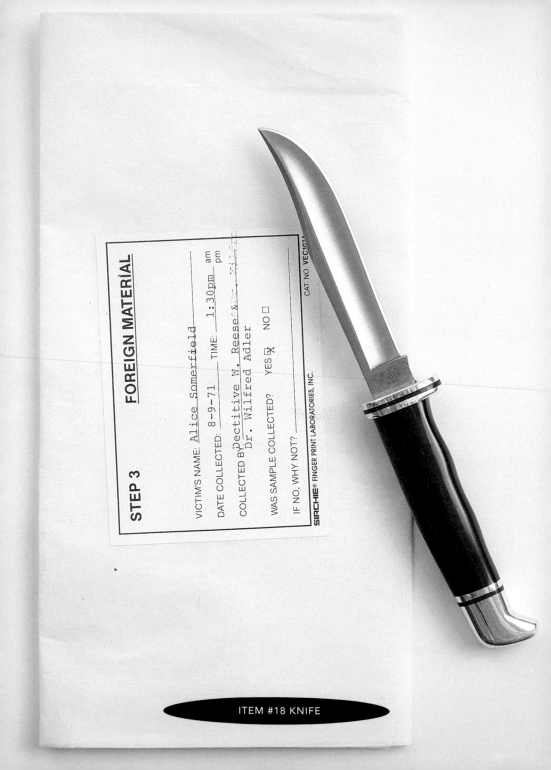

STEP 3

<u>FOREIGN MATERIAL</u>

VICTIM'S NAME: Alice Somerfield

DATE COLLECTED: 8-9-71   TIME: 1:30pm am/pm

COLLECTED BY: Dective W. Reese & Dr. Wilfred

Dr. Wilfred Adler

WAS SAMPLE COLLECTED?   YES ☒   NO ☐

IF NO, WHY NOT?

SIRCHIE® FINGER PRINT LABORATORIES, INC.   CAT. NO. VEC102

ITEM #18 KNIFE

FD-263

FEDERAL BUREAU OF INVESTIGATION

REPORTING OFFICE	OFFICE OF ORIGIN	DATE	INVESTIGATIVE PERIOD
Albany, NY	Albany, NY	8-28-71	August ███

TITLE OF CASE	REPORT MADE BY	TYPED BY
Appendix A	Special Agent K. Willers	A.M.H.

CHARACTER OF CASE An elaboration on the novel The End Of Alice, exploring ████ the process of creating a character and the building of a fiction.

Appendix A contains the clues which permitted the author into the narrator's mind--becoming archetypical icons for the narrator's imagination. A book of physical evidence, the appendix documents the items one imagines the narrator hid during his twenty-three years of incarceration, remnants of his relationship with a little girl called Alice; teeth, ███████, watch, ███████, ████, letters from his correspondents, various forms and his photo album. This scrapbook, collected by the author during the five years it took to write The End Of Alice, is illustrative of not only key events in the narrator's life, but of the fluidity and fragmentation of identity and functions much like a photo insert in a true crime paperback--a kind of liquid proof. And finally there are the paintings, incorporating elements of collage; the photographs, the physical evidence, the text. Translating voice into gesture, the paintings are a further articulation of the life of a character, an investigation of the act of writing a novel such as ███████, and ultimately an amalgam of both the character's impulses and the author's experience of the novel.

APPROVED _____ SPECIAL AGENT IN CHARGE _____ DO NOT WRITE IN SPACES BELOW

COPIES MADE
4500 published by San Francisco Art Space; distributed by DAP

FBI CASE REPORT

Dissemination Record of Attached Report					Notations copies to:
Agency	X				Anne MacDonald
Request Recd.	bc				Maureen Keefe
Date Fwd.	8-30-71				Kristin Johnson
How Fwd.	cert				Sarah Chalfant
By	KW				Jamie Wolf

COVER PAGE

FBI/DOJ

August 2, 1994

I knew who you are and I knew what you did.
Your footsteps are deep and leave tracks like mud.
Do you even have a clue? My reason for writing was
that I thought it might make me less afraid if I
could talk to you, if I could find out who you really
are, what makes you tick. What does it mean for a girl
like me to write to you? Do you like it? Do you
like it a lot? Am I torturing you? I have to be honest
with you and plus, there's not a lot to lose. And what
are you going to do anyway—come kill me?

My life is completely different because of you.
I doubt you realise it but your influence is everywhere
And it'd not only me, it, 'd all the mothers and All the
girls. Everyone is afraid. I wasn't allowed to play in
the front yard, "Out back," my mother would say, "Play
in the backyard, it's fenced, no one needs to know we
have a little girl. No one needs to know anything." She
said it as though my playing on the front lawn was an
advertisement for things that might be taken from my
parents house, burgled. And, I couldn't walk to school
alone, they were afraid I'd evaporate, disappear right
off the sidewalk, that the sidewalk itself was the path
that led straight to men like you. "And never go in the
woods alone," my mother said. I never knew if that was

because you&d be there, hiding in your secret
headquarters or if it was for fear of what I'd find--
the forest is your burial ground.

Keep an eye out. Report anything strange. They say a
man like you can be anyone, someone I know, someone I
trust, a friend of the family, a relative or even the
mailman. How do I know which one is you? What are your
distinguishing characteristics? What makes you different
from everyone else? Do you walk with a limp? Have scars?
Leer? Will I feel you coming up behind me? Will your
fingers reach round and cover my mouth? How do you pick
your girls? Do you look as crazy as you are? And why do
you hate me? Or more, specifically, why do you hate
little girls?

August 9, 1934

It's so hot today that I'm sticking to myself. Do
you have a/c in your cell? We8ve got central but today
even that's not enough. So, what's new? There are
things I should probably be telling you--details, like
I drive to Sing Sing--a lot. I hang out on the hill at
State street by the fire station. From there you can
hear the noise,inside the prison, you can hear the men.
Last time I took Matt with me and he totally freaked,
he kept saying, " I don't want to see any people, whatever you do, don't make me see the people." There are
trailets in the back, weird little Winnebego's where I guess the
guards live and out front there's a parking place reserved
for the "employee of the month." Bet you didn't know that.
More still, Last week, I drove myself to the motel in
Chatham. I told my mother I was going to visit a friend
from school. I slept in the room you did it in. I asked
the housekeeper which one it was and had the manager
switch me. There was no hint, no sign that anything had
ever happened. And yet, I could feel you. I could feel
you everywhere. I live differently because of you--there
is no such thing as safety.

Hey, are you allowed visitors? How would it be if like
maybe sometime I came to see you--would it be okay?

KNOWN BLOOD SAMPLES

STEP 12

ORAL SWABS AND SMEARS

STEP 9

RECTAL SWABS AND SMEARS

STEP 8

VAGINAL SWABS AND SMEARS

STEP 7

STEP 6   PULLED PUBIC HAIRS

VICTIM'S NAME: _____Alice Somerfield_____

DATE COLLECTED: __8-9-71_____ TIME: __1:30 pm_____ am
                                                           pm

COLLECTED BY Dr. Wilfred Adler_____

WAS SAMPLE COLLECTED?   YES XX   NO ☐

IF NO, WHY NOT? _____

SIRCHIE® FINGER PRINT LABORATORIES, INC.   CAT. NO. VEC106

SAMPLES AND SMEARS

A YELLOW TRUCK

3. **Sex Crime and Prison Punishment**

by Robert Johnson

S ex offenders, especially violent sex offenders, have a special need to face and work through their personal problems, problems that are intense and deep-seated, and usually rooted in traumatic childhood sexual abuse experienced in the family. Prison is especially inhospitable to them, for in prison denial is the norm. Admission of any weakness and inadequacy is met with hostile rejection. Sex offenders harbor human failings that are, by any reckoning, profound and perverse. They typically hate themselves more, often much more, than others would or could hate them, even if others came to know the depths of their depravity. Hence the only real means of psychological survival open to these offenders is to deny as fully and completely as possible the horrible things they have done, things that nevertheless percolate below the surface of their minds, tormenting them, relegating them to a life in which defenses and denials and even delusions must be tended to, like a fine and fragile garden, on an almost continuous basis if they are to maintain even the appearance of a normal life.

Sex offenders are clustered together in some prisons; in others, they are mixed in with regular offenders. In either instance, they gravitate to others—the weak and impaired—who live on the margins of the prison community. For in the eyes of the hard-core convicts, sex offenders, and especially those who victimize children, are the lowest of the low. Commonly, they are treated with outright contempt and even violence, including sexual violence. Often, this rejection is played out, in miniature, in the atrophied social world sex offenders develop among themselves.

More than other offenders, sex criminals need a respite from themselves and from the prison world. But for them there is no escape. All too often, prison offers sex offenders a world that is shrunk down to the confines of the cell. Monsters to others and to themselves, in prison they typically live alone, for weeks and months and even years at a time, in cells that are at once a haven from the rejection of other prisoners but also a trap, a kind of existential void in which they become prisoners yet again in a psychic wasteland informed by their own tortured fantasies. For many, the line between fantasy and reality blurs. They live on the raw edge of repressed urges; the bare walls of prison cells serve as screens on which to project their secret yearnings and worst nightmares.

More than anything else, sex offenders desperately need a reprieve from the constant press of sexuality which haunts them mercilessly. The prison would seem at first blush to be a sterile, sexless environment— the Quakers and others who touted the rehabilitative value of the original penitentiaries certainly supposed it to be—but nothing could be further from the truth. The aura of sexuality is pervasive. Hard-bodied men, bare-chested, pump iron in the prison yard, sporting flamboyant tattoos; lines of naked men proceed to and from showers. Rapes, including semi-public group rapes known as "trains," pose a lingering threat, especially to the pariahs of the prison community. Sex offenders, of course, top the roster of sexual targets.

In men's prisons, sexual deprivation dominates the pains of imprisonment, shaping—and warping human interaction, imparting a distinctive surly edge to much of the give and take of prison life. Sexual hunger seeps into the cells, where it pools and then sours in the pictures of loved ones, real and fantasized, drawn from personal albums or pornographic magazines, in either instance prominently displayed on cell walls; and in the acrid, musky smells that offer telltale signs of male loneliness. Here, in cages that offer a hideaway from other prisoners but still leave men exposed to the sexual dimensions of prison life, sex offenders make their home. Here, their fantasy worlds—worlds often featuring pains and perversions, ugly memories inching their way toward the edges of consciousness—threaten to rule their thoughts. Here, alone and unaided, they must carve out a life for themselves.

Sex offenders are profoundly and uniquely lonely in prison. Cast out from the larger society, cast off from the prison society, alienated even from themselves, they are utterly alone. For them, contact or correspondence with others in the outside world takes on great allure. They are needy, and hence vulnerable. Contact with the outside world provides a vehicle for fantasy which is valued, but also a bridge into repressed thoughts and feelings, which they struggle to suppress. Perhaps for these offenders, as for long-term inmates generally, survival comes easiest when the barren, spartan world of the prison, hemmed in by its vast and unfeeling walls, forms the limit of their human consciousness.

September 11, 1995

Robert Johnson, Ph.D.
Professor and Chair, Department of Justice, Law and Society
The American University
Washington, D.C.

ARTSPACE BOOKS IS A FORUM FOR
CONTEMPORARY ARTISTS AND WRITERS.
THESE COLLABORATIONS OF
IMAGE AND TEXT BY TODAY'S MOST
INNOVATIVE ARTISTS CHALLENGE THE
CULTURE IN WHICH WE LIVE,
AND INSCRIBE THE VITAL SOCIAL
FUNCTION OF ART.

PREVIOUSLY RELEASED FROM
ARTSPACE BOOKS:

MEMORIES THAT SMELL LIKE GASOLINE
BY DAVID WOJNAROWICZ

JERK
ART BY NAYLAND BLAKE
FICTION BY DENNIS COOPER

REAL GONE
ART BY JACK PIERSON
FICTION BY JIM LEWIS

DESIRE BY NUMBERS
ART BY NAN GOLDIN
FICTION BY KLAUS KERTESS

THE STRANGE CASE OF T.L.
ART BY TONY LABAT
TEXT BY CARLO McCORMICK

Evidence of Other Ejaculation:

1 ☐ No
2 ☐ On Body of Victim

There Is Evidence to Suggest Postm

2

1 ☐ Yes

. Is There Evidence of Sexual Inserti
Body?

1 ☐ Yes

6. Evidence of Sexual Insertion of Fo
(e.g., rocks, twigs, knife, clothing):
(object)

1 ☐ Vagina _____

2 ☐ Penis _____

3 ☐ Anus _____

77. There Is Evidence of Sexual Inser
Not In The Body When the Bod

1 ☐ Yes ── _____ (descr